GROUNDHOG GRACE

In a burrow,
deep beneath the earth,
Lived a groundhog, Grace,
sleeping for all she was worth.

She was timid and shy,
but one fine day,
The humans chose her
to say yay or nay.

But her cousin Wally,
had something to say.
He wanted the glory
on Groundhog Day,
"I can't believe
they chose you instead,
I'm older and stronger
and better," he said.

Grace lay in her burrow,
her mind in a spin,
"How can I predict anything?
How do I begin?"
Her nerves were frazzled,
her mind in a whirl.
"And is Wally just angry
because I'm a girl?"

She knew she had to talk
to someone wise,
So she went to her Grandpa,
under starlit skies.
"Grandpa, I'm so worried
about the big day,
What if I'm late,
or do it the wrong way?"

"What if I fall over?
What if I get sick?
What if my shadow
plays me a trick?"
There really was no end
to her worries.
Grandpa could see
she was anxious and flurried.

Grandpa smiled gently,
and patted her head,
"Grace, my dear child,
you have nothing to dread.
I'm so proud of you.
It's an honor to be chosen.
Best to go home and sleep now.
Your paws will be frozen."

"Just believe in yourself,
and do your best,
And if things don't go as
planned,
don't stress!
Sometimes things happen,
that are out of our hands,
Try, that's all that matters,
Grace. Please understand."

With Grandpa's wise words,
Grace felt better,
She promised to follow
his advice to the letter.
She kissed his cheek,
and said with conviction,
"I'll make you proud,
with my weather prediction!"

The following day was Groundhog Day morning, Grace found her jitters had disappeared without warning. She spoke to herself kindly, "Grace, just do your best, Mother Nature will take care of the rest!"

Into the february morning,
Grace emerged with care,
But cousin Wally, the bully,
had beaten her there.

He had tampered with the rocks
and tree roots outside,
so that Grace took a tumble
and ended up on her backside.

With no first glance at her shadow,
she knew she had been tricked,
Long winter or early spring was
impossible to predict,

Grace turned to the humans
and shrugged.
She wished she could voice
That she wasn't responsible
for her cousin's poor choice.

The humans were all
understanding and kind,
Wally felt guilty
for the trick he'd designed.
He apologized to Grace
and learned his lesson,
That winning isn't always
a healthy obsession.

Grace may not
have predicted the weather,
But she did her best,
and that is much better.
She learned to believe in herself,
to stand up and try,
And that's a valuable life lesson
we can all live by.

Thanks for reading about Grace the groundhog.

I hope you believe in yourself when you are faced with something you are trying for the first time.

Grace believes in you!

Made in the USA
Las Vegas, NV
26 January 2024

84884771R00021